Bridget's

TOM LICHTENHELD

Christy Ottaviano Books

HENRY HOLT AND COMPANY, NEW YORK

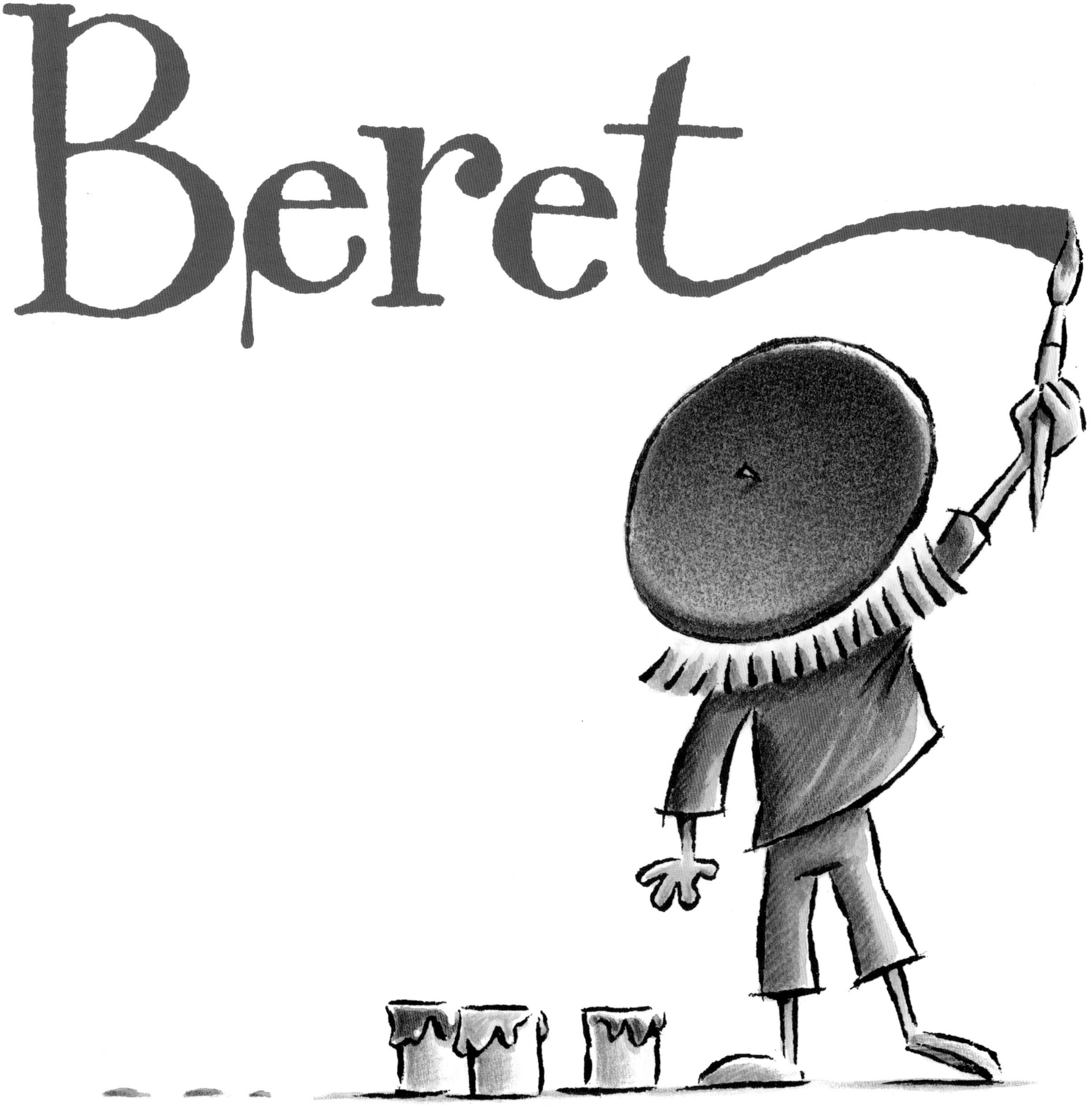
Beret

Bridget was drawn to drawing.
She liked to draw as much as other
kids liked ice cream.

Her favorite place to draw was outdoors.
When she was outdoors, drawing all the
things around her, Bridget felt like she was
right where she belonged.

Did somebody
say "ice cream"?

She created many masterpieces.
Some went on permanent exhibit.

Others were only available for limited viewing.

Of course, Bridget had lots of art supplies, but her most important art supply wasn't something to draw or paint with. It was a hat.

Not just any old hat, but a big black beret. The kind of hat that lots of Great Artists wear.

Before Bridget made any kind of art, she'd put on her beret and adjust it until it looked just right. It had to have that certain *je ne sais quoi*. She had no idea what that meant, but she knew all Great Artists needed it to make art.

One day, just as Bridget was putting an inspired dash of purple on a cluster of flowers, a big gust of wind came along and lifted her beret right off her head. It caught the breeze . . .

Unfortunately, this kite didn't have a string. All it had was a little girl running after it, screaming, "My beret! My beret!"

... and went sailing through the air like a kite.

Before Bridget could even get over the fence, her beret was out of sight.

She searched the neighborhood, asking everyone if they had seen her beret.

She filed a Missing Beret Report.

She even offered a reward.

But it was no use. Bridget had lost her beret.
And with it, she was sure, her ability to draw.

She tried on all the other hats in the house, to see if any of them would give her artistic inspiration.

A Cowboy Hat

Draw, partner!

A FEZ

Do I have to be in a parade?

A PROPELLER BEANIE

How uplifting.

A COONSKIN CAP

Gross.

A PITH HELMET

I have to go to the bathroom.

Dad's fishing hat

P.U.!

But she wasn't the least bit inspired by any of them.

So Bridget gave up, and did what any self-respecting artist would do.

She cried.

And pouted.

And sulked.

And generally felt
sorry for herself.

Her friend Madeline invited her to draw,
but Bridget said, "I can't draw, I have artist's block."

"I have blocks, too," said Madeline,
"but I can still draw."

If you don't feel like drawing, or can't think of something to draw, you might have artist's block. It's not fatal, but it is annoying. Here are a few ways to cure it.

1 MAKE UP A FUNNY ANIMAL.

2 DRAW PEOPLE WITH FUNNY HAIR.

3 DRAW SOMETHING REALLY BIG!

4 MAKE A SCRIBBLE, THEN TURN IT INTO SOMETHING.

A few days later, her little sister Jessie asked her,
"Bridget, would you please make a sign for our lemonade stand?"

"I can't," said Bridget, "I don't have my beret."

"But it's not a drawing, it's just
a sign," said Jessie.
"Puhleeease?"

"Well, okay, I'll make your sign,"
Bridget replied grumpily,
"but no drawing."

Bridget got a big roll of paper,
some paint and brushes,
and began to make a sign.

Did somebody say "lemonade"?
That would be good with ICE CREAM!

She couldn't help but notice that, with a little bit of yellow paint,
the "O" in the word "lemonade" could become a lemon.
And it needed a little bump at the bottom. And a leaf. Or two.

"And I'd better put a smiling face over here, so everyone
will know the girls at this lemonade stand are friendly."

There were still some empty spaces on the sign.
She filled those in with other shapes and colors
that looked a lot like drawings.

"That's an okay sign," said Bridget,
"but you'll need another one down at
the corner to attract customers."

"And another one for the other corner…"

I already had the paint poured anyway.

Before she knew it, Bridget was painting signs
as fast as the girls could put them up.

Pretty soon, every tree, telephone pole, and signpost in the neighborhood held one of Bridget's masterpieces.

All the neighbors thought it was a wonderful art opening.

They gathered around the refreshment table
to discuss the paintings and how great it was that
Bridget was able to make art again.

"Where is Bridget, anyway?" they wondered.

She was right back where she belonged.

FOR MADELINE

*Bridget's artwork is based on drawings by Jack Barrie, Charlotte Lichtenheld,
Johanna Lichtenheld, Zoey Lichtenheld, Emily Lichtenheld, Lily Byrne Osuch,
Preston Sullivan, Jessie Zenz, and Madeline Zenz.*

*Thanks to Christian Golden for storyline advice and to my colleagues
at Cramer-Krasselt for their flexibility*

As always, with love and deepest gratitude to my wife, Jan

PERMISSION TO REPRODUCE THE FOLLOWING WORKS OF ART IS GRATEFULLY ACKNOWLEDGED:

Giuseppe Arcimboldo (1527–93), *Summer*, 1573 (oil on canvas) / Private Collection / © Agnew's, London, UK / The Bridgeman Art Library
International; Mary Cassatt (1845–1926), *Child with a Red Hat*, c.1908 (pastel on paper) / Sterling and Francine Clark Art Institute, Williamstown,
MA, USA / The Bridgeman Art Library International; Paul Cézanne (1839–1906), *Still Life with Peaches and Pears*, c.1890 (oil on canvas) / ©
The Barnes Foundation, Merion, PA, USA / The Bridgeman Art Library International; Vincent van Gogh (1853–90), *Bedroom at Arles*, 1889 (oil
on canvas) / Art Institute of Chicago, IL, USA / The Bridgeman Art Library International; Henri Matisse (1869–1954), *Icarus*, plate VIII from
the Jazz series, 1947 (pochoir plate) / © 2009 Succession H. Matisse / Artists Rights Society (ARS), NY / Photo: Archives Matisse; Claude
Monet (1840–1926), *Still Life with Sunflowers*, 1880 (oil on canvas) / Metropolitan Museum of Art, New York, NY, USA / The Bridgeman Art
Library International; Georgia O'Keeffe (1887–1986), *Above the Clouds I*, 1962–63 (oil on canvas, 36 1/8 x 48 1/4 in. 1997.05.14) / Gift of the Burnett
Foundation and The Georgia O'Keeffe Foundation / Photo: Malcolm Varon 2001 / Location: The Georgia O'Keeffe Museum, Santa Fe, NM,
USA / © 2009 Georgia O'Keeffe Museum / Artists Rights Society (ARS), NY; Pablo Picasso (1881–1973), *Bull's Head* (assemblage, bicycle seat and
handle bars, 33.5 x 43.5 x 19 cm. MP330) / Photo: Beatrice Hatala / Location: Musée Picasso, Paris, France / © 2009 Estate of Pablo Picasso /
Artists Rights Society (ARS), NY; Rembrandt Harmensz van Rijn (1606–69), *Self-Portrait in a Cap, Open-Mouthed*, 1630 (etching, 51 x 46 mm, B.320,
II. Inv. RvR 442) / The Pierpont Morgan Library, New York, NY, USA; Georges Seurat (1859–91), *Sunday Afternoon on the Island of La Grande Jatte*,
1884–86 (oil on canvas) / Art Institute of Chicago, IL, USA / The Bridgeman Art Library International; Alfred Sisley (1839–99), *The Boat in the
Flood, Port-Marly*, 1876 (oil on canvas) / Musée d'Orsay, Paris, France / The Bridgeman Art Library International.

Henry Holt and Company, LLC, *Publishers since 1866*
175 Fifth Avenue, New York, New York 10010 (www.HenryHoltKids.com)

Henry Holt® is a registered trademark of Henry Holt and Company, LLC.

Library of Congress Cataloging-in-Publication Data
Lichtenheld, Tom. Bridget's beret / by Tom Lichtenheld. — 1st ed.   p.   cm.
"Christy Ottaviano Books."
Summary: When Bridget loses the beret that provides her with artistic inspiration like other great artists,
she thinks she will never be able to draw again.
ISBN 978-0-8050-8775-8
[1. Drawing—Fiction. 2. Artists—Fiction. 3. Hats—Fiction. 4. Self-confidence—Fiction.] I. Title.
PZ7.L592Br 2010   [E]—dc22   2009012220

First Edition—2010
The illustrations for this book were created in ink, colored pencil, watercolor,
and sidewalk chalk on 80-pound Strathmore Aquarius watercolor paper. The display type is hand-lettered.
Printed in January 2010 in China by South China Printing Co. Ltd.,
Dongguan City, Guangdong Province, on acid-free paper. ∞

1 3 5 7 9 10 8 6 4 2

Turn the page
to check out
Bridget's ideas
for artistic
inspiration.

How to Start Your Art

Try these Bridget-approved ideas for inspiring yourself, based on techniques used by many famous beret-wearing artists.

Make Faces

Rembrandt van Rijn (1606–1669) was a Dutch artist who practiced by making faces in the mirror and drawing himself. (Here, he seems to be saying "OMG!") You and your friends can draw each other expressing surprise, anger, happiness, and other emotions.

The Pierpont Morgan Library / Art Resource, NY

Paint Lots of Dots

French artist Georges Seurat (1859–1891) invented a technique called pointillism, which is simply painting with many dots of color. Using crayons, see if you can make a picture by just making lots of dots.

Draw a "Head" of Lettuce

Italian artist Giuseppe Arcimboldo (1527–1593) liked to paint people made out of vegetables. He probably just did it to avoid eating his broccoli and carrots. "Mom, I can't eat this broccoli because I have to use it as a model for my friend's head!" Draw your friends as if they were made of vegetables, then call your new art form "vegetablism."

Go to Your Room, Then Draw It

Dutch artist Vincent van Gogh (1853–1890) painted this picture to show two things: 1. how good he was at painting his room; 2. how good he was at cleaning his room. By the way, van Gogh is pronounced van Gahk. When said correctly it sounds like you're gagging on a prune.

When All Else Fails, Use Red!

This painting by American-born artist Mary Cassatt (1845–1926) demonstrates the power of color, and nothing's more powerful than a big ol' glob of red. Try drawing with just red or some other bright color.

Get Your Head in the Clouds

Alfred Sisley (1839–1899) was a French painter who was excellent at painting clouds. Do a drawing that's nothing but clouds. See how many shapes you can make. See how many shades of blue you can create. See if you can paint clouds that look like they're moving across the sky.

Pablo Picasso (1881–1973) was a Spanish artist who turned ordinary things into art, like these bicycle parts he made into a bull's head. See if you can find some junk around the house and turn it into a work of art.

Turn Old Junk . . .

. . . into Great Art

Cut It Out!

Henri Matisse (1869–1954) was a French artist who created beautiful paper collages. He called it "painting with scissors." Try putting away your paints and crayons and using colored paper and scissors instead.

Go Forth and Be a Fruitful Artist

French artist Paul Cézanne (1839–1906) painted lots of fruit—probably because it sits still and doesn't complain. Set up a still life with your favorite fruits, then try not to eat the still life before you're done painting it.

Discover Flower Power

You can't go wrong with flowers. French artist Claude Monet (1840–1926) loved to paint flowers so much he turned his whole yard into a flower garden. Pick your favorite flowers and see how many ways you can paint them.

Look at Things Differently

American artist Georgia O'Keeffe (1887–1986) did this painting of clouds from above after her first ride in an airplane. Try looking at something ordinary from a new angle and drawing it that way. For instance, what does a chair look like from underneath?

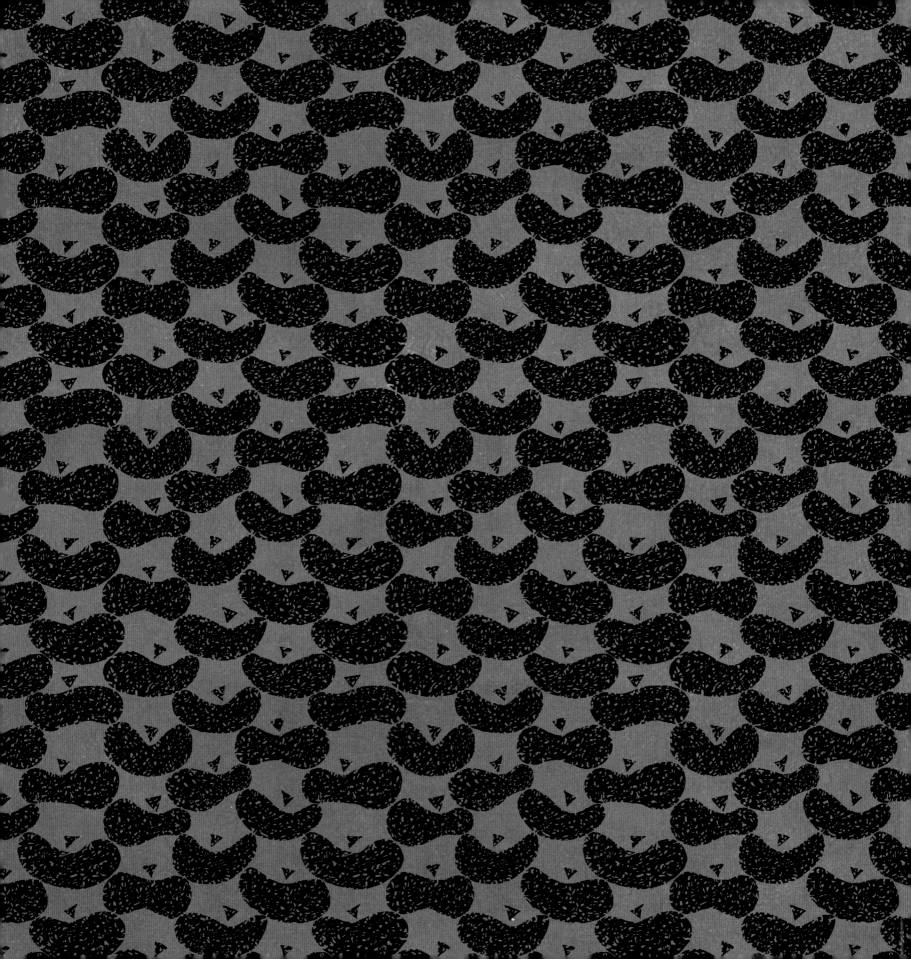